MASTERING THE ART OF DECISION MAKING

Mastering the Art of Decision Making
How to Make the Best Choices in Life
By Tejgyan Global Foundation

Copyright © Tejgyan Global Foundation
All Rights Reserved 2018

Tejgyan Global Foundation is a charitable organization
with its headquarters in Pune, India.

Published by WOW Publishings Pvt. Ltd., India

First edition published in May 2018

Copyrights are reserved with Tejgyan Global Foundation and publishing rights are vested exclusively with WOW Publishings Pvt. Ltd. This book is sold subject to the condition that it shall not by way of trade or otherwise, be lent, resold, hired out, or otherwise circulated without the publisher's prior written consent in any form of binding or cover other than that in which it is published and without a similar condition including this condition being imposed on the subsequent purchaser and without limiting the rights under copyright reserved above, no part of this publication may be reproduced, stored in or introduced into a retrieval system, or transmitted, in any form, or by any means, electronic, mechanical, photocopying, recording or otherwise, without the prior written permission of both the copyright owner and the above-mentioned publisher of this book. Any person who does any unauthorized act in relation to this publication may be liable to criminal prosecution and civil claims for damages.

To those,
who have positively touched the lives of many
by being responsible and committed to their decisions.

Contents

1. Key Considerations for Decision Making / 11
2. Tools for Effective Decisions / 22
3. Qualities Required for Making Effective Decisions / 32
4. Collective Decision Making in a Group / 46
5. Guidance through Intuition / 53
6. Decisions from Higher Consciousness / 63
7. Making the Highest Choice / 72
8. Decision Meditation / 81

Preface

In the Indian epic, the Mahabharata, Arjuna lays down his weapons in the battlefield, being seized by despondency. He falls into the abyss of confusion, fear, and anguish. He refuses to wage the war against his beloved elders and cites various logical reasons for renouncing the battlefield.

At this juncture, Lord Krishna expounds the profound wisdom of the Bhagavad Gita. He raises Arjuna's awareness and throws light on his ignorance. In this light of wisdom, Arjuna gains a life transforming perspective about how to act in the various situations that life brings up. With the renewed understanding, he gets up, rejuvenated, and takes up his arms to fight the war of righteousness.

It is so striking that a valiant warrior, the best of his times, lays down his weapons and wishes to escape the battle. Being held in the clutches of a weak mind, his resolve quivers and he is prepared to run away from the very battle that he was eager to fight.

Even more striking is the 180° shift in his decision after receiving divine guidance from Lord Krishna. This also shows the powerful impact that true wisdom can have on one's decisions. True wisdom enlightens us on who we really are. It throws light on the false assumptions that we have been living by.

We make decisions from morning till night. From the first thing in the morning, where many people decide whether to get up or sleep for some more time to the many domestic decisions of the homemaker – what needs to be prepared for breakfast or lunch, when to go shopping, when the children need to complete their homework etc.

Youngsters need to choose their career or business. They need to decide when to get married and settle down. Teachers need to decide what to teach the students and how. Doctors and lawyers draw judgements for health and social scenarios. Their choices have a bearing on people's lives.

Corporates need to make decisions that affect the businesses of their clients, the lives and careers of their employees, and also their shareholder value. The government needs to make complex decisions regarding the nation's economy, security, foreign policy etc. At this level, decisions can drive strategies, can be tactical, influencing the short-to-medium term, or operational day-to-day decisions.

The consequences of decisions we make cannot always be predicted with full accuracy. Hence, many decisions involve risks, which need to be clearly understood to help make the most appropriate choices from available options.

Given these challenges, decision making is a key capability that all of us, without exception, need to develop. We need to take responsibility for the choices we make, even if their consequences are undesirable.

Our decisions shape our lives. We can experience a favorable future only if we make the right choices at key junctures in our lives. Ironically, though this subject is so vital, we do not see it being taught in most schools.

This book reveals some deep aspects about decision making that are relevant to every one of us, regardless of our stage of life, whether we are a student, a homemaker or a business-owner, an employee or a professional. It addresses the key considerations that determine how we develop ourselves to take effective decisions.

Congratulations on deciding to read this book!

1

Key Considerations for Decision Making

For most people, taking decisions turns out to be a mechanical process. There are as many styles of decision-making as there are people. The decisions of each one are influenced by the choices that they have made in their past. Past choices, that people have made, keep repeating mechanically in their lives.

There are certain aspects that can be brought into the way we take decisions, which can make our decisions more conscious, informed and appropriate. Let us look at some key considerations that can help us make more conscious, novel and responsible choices.

Avoid escaping decisions

People tend to avoid decisions owing to the fear of failure or the fear of an undesirable outcome. They lack the courage to make mistakes and take responsibility for the outcomes.

Such avoidance does not help to make better choices in the future. Not taking decisions, or rather, the avoidance of having to make a decision, is also a decision that brings its consequence.

We can decide not to make a decision right now, but it should be a conscious decision to postpone a decision after careful thought.

We cannot escape making decisions. Whether we postpone our choice, or avoid choosing, we are already deciding one way or the other. It is only by taking decisions that one can learn the art of decision making.

When one lacks confidence in making choices for oneself, it is likely that they will lose faith in themselves, affecting other areas of their lives. It can cause them to lose their ability to face life's challenges and overcome limitations.

Each one of us has immense potential that can be unleashed in life. The power we hold is reflected in our ability to choose what is right for us. When we choose to escape making decisions, we do not realize that we are actually giving up control over our lives. If we are unwilling to make decisions, others will decide for us.

Hence, we need to start taking small decisions, so as to develop confidence. In the process, we will release our fear of decision-making and learn to take major decisions as well.

Don't depend on others for your decisions

Suppose one finds it difficult to choose clothes for oneself and hence one always buys clothes by consulting others. Here, one has the opportunity to choose clothes for themselves. It may so happen that people criticize their choices, but one need not be disappointed. In the case of clothes, 'one-size-fits-all' never works. You should choose what fits right for you.

We live in a commoditized world where outsourced services are taking over major functions of our lives. We try to minimize the consumption of our time and effort by outsourcing as many facets of our lives as possible. This has led to a world where increasingly many things that one could do, or rather should be doing themselves, are available as services provided in exchange for money. As a result, we tend to shed our responsibility of making choices for ourselves, and transferring the onus and also the risks to others. Unfortunately, others often choose what they believe is good for them, assuming that the same will work for us.

Our education system tends to teach students to fit everything into 'right' or 'wrong' silos. This stifles the originality in the students' thought process. Their brains are wired to think that there are only certain fixed ways or answers to tackle life situations.

Most people are the product of such education and lead lives based on fixed beliefs handed down by the educational system. Their decisions reflect these beliefs. They rely on authority and follow the herd instinct.

People will always have a variety of opinions that are true only for themselves. Knowing this, you can allow people to comment and criticize. This does not mean that you don't heed the opinions of others. While you give a careful thought to their opinions as inputs for your contemplation, you can learn to make the right choice for yourself only by taking independent decisions.

You may seek advice or suggestions from people, but stop being compelled to borrow others' choices. With this, comes the responsibility for your choices. Your choices may turn out to be mistaken. But as long as you ensure that you are learning from the outcomes of your decisions, you only make progress.

Delegate what is not important

We just discussed about the damaging habit of transferring the responsibility for our decisions onto others. Having said that, we also need to carefully assess which decisions are important and have to be taken by ourselves. We should save our time and energy for the newer and more important decisions.

We need not be involved in every trivial decision. We can hand over the responsibility of certain decisions that are of routine everyday significance to others. We can perhaps delegate such tasks to our family or staff at the workplace or assistants. In this way, we can save the time and energy for bigger and more important decisions.

It is the responsibility of the decision-maker to consider how the decision should be implemented appropriately. Decision and its responsibility go hand in hand.

Avoid giving excuses for not taking decisions

We generally tend to postpone decisions because deciding would require us to begin with something new. People generally resist change. The law of inertia applies to the mind too. The mind likes to continue to do things in the same manner in which one has been doing.

Till the time one decides, one continues to live in the same manner. The day one decides to do something different, their daily routine changes. When you try something new, you need to find time to prepare for it.

If we resist change, we will try to escape it and remain in our comfort zone. For example, when we decide to lead a healthy life, our activities and our food habits have to undergo a change. With this decision, there is change in our daily routine. We may need to form new habits, which may not be palatable to the tongue.

Initially, the mind always resists change. The mind desires comforts and convenience and hence, remains snug the cocoon of its comfort zone. Anything that challenges the mind and shakes it out of its comfort zone is resisted. This very habit of resisting acts as a block in decision making. We should not be a slave to this inertia of the mind.

In order to escape decisions and avoid the consequent changes, people often give various excuses or reasons for not starting something or completing something. The consequences of their indecision do not just affect them, but also others concerned.

Giving good reasons or excuses does not complete the job. They are only ways of avoiding responsibility. On the face of it, one may be convinced that the excuses are genuine reasons, and yet, they really do not help the end-goal.

For example, when people are called in to work at a certain time, they arrive late and give excuses that they missed the bus. They may even quote bizarre reasons like they could not wake up on time because the clock stopped and hence the alarm did not sound!

Before giving reasons, we need to honestly contemplate whether they are genuine reasons or lame excuses to escape work. When we contemplate honestly, it is possible that we may discover a need to train our body and mind. By presenting excuses, we only avoid shouldering responsibility.

We can inculcate discipline and strengthen our character by following a 'No blame and No excuses' policy. Avoid blaming anyone to hide our mistakes and if some work is not completed, face it honestly instead of looking for excuses.

A trained person completes the most challenging of tasks despite numerous difficulties. The more you heat gold, the more it glitters. In the same way, when you repeatedly decide to complete any work and follow it up with appropriate action, your body and mind also get trained.

Timely decisions

There is right time for everything. In the same way, there is right time for taking a decision and also for not taking it. This is when you recognize the opportunity. When you take a right decision at the right time, you find that it is effective.

For example, if a university student considers getting married before completing his studies, he needs to assess whether he will be able to continue to focus on his studies thereafter. If he senses a risk, he should decide to first concentrate on his studies. He can then decide to become financially independent. When he becomes capable of shouldering the responsibilities of a family, then he can decide to get married.

Making the right decision at the wrong time is as ineffective as making the wrong decision at the right time. We should contemplate and conclude the right decision in good time. Take the right decision at the right time. This also means making the decision within a given time period.

For everyday decisions, we need not give too much thought. But for decisions that have a major bearing on our medium and long term lives, we need to decide a time-limit to make a decision. So first decide, by when you will decide.

Deciding a time-limit helps in avoiding unnecessary hurrying or procrastination. It also helps in avoiding spending too much time in analysis that leads to paralysis of the mind! You are aware of when you need to give the decision your attention.

Timely decisions do not necessarily mean speedy decisions. It means the decision is made in an appropriate amount of time. At times, it could be immediate, while at times, it could take a week.

Never decide in haste. Even if at times there is a need to decide in haste, choose an option which can be reversed or corrected later. When we know that our decision cannot be reversed, we should carefully give time, attention and thinking. Never decide impulsively in haste, just to escape thinking, or by quoting the excuse of insufficient time. Let not lethargy, procrastination, or haste influence your decisions, ever.

Fine thinking

In this age of ever-increasing speed and chaos, people tend to jump to conclusions and make decisions impulsively, based on superficial data and old patterns of success. It is not too much of a stretch to say that fine thinking is rarely used in decision making.

Fine thinking enables you to approach your decisions from

various angles, which may not necessarily have been thought of earlier. It helps reveal hidden aspects that you would otherwise have never known.

Fine thinking can also be called subtle thinking. It demands a deep reflection on subtle details of factors that influence the decision. It is a technique by which we ignore no point, however tangential, until we reach its core.

While deciding, one should choose one from the available options. Another possible approach is to choose a middle path, which combines two or more options together. Options that vary in their approach, but lead to a common desirable outcome, can be potentially combined together to bring the merits of multiple options together.

Rehearse the choices mentally, even better in written form, so that you can pre-empt the scenarios that can arise when you proceed with each of the options available. With this approach of contemplating decision options, depth is more important than the breadth of coverage. Those who are able to do Fine thinking can achieve tremendous success through the choices they make in their lives.

One effective way to reveal subtler or hidden nuances of the choices is the 5W technique. This technique consists of asking five generic questions in the context of a given decision – What, Why, How, Who and When. These questions are powerful means to develop a higher perspective and deeper understanding of the decision scenario.

When we try to practice fine thinking mentally, our thoughts can take us round in circles. When conflicting thoughts arise, without being observed and audited, they can lead us in unwanted directions, lead us to false conclusions.

Hence, it is essential to write down the thread of thoughts, so that we do not lose track of our thoughts as they go out of control. The practice of focused writing can really help in gaining clarity of the decision scenario. It helps us audit and observe our own thoughts in a detached manner.

Nurture the quality of Foresight

Foresight is an essential quality that ensures good decisions. With foresight, we can prepare for future possibilities today.

For example, if the body starts showing signs of wear and tear through symptoms of pain or illness, with foresight, we can recognize these signs of imminent ill-health and take corrective action before a full-blown disease develops. Perhaps we'll begin with an exercise regimen, make changes to our diet or lifestyle. Similarly, if we are mentally stressed, we can introspect and practice silence through meditation. As a result, we regain our mental balance and become healthier emotionally.

If we aspire to create a happy and self-sufficient society, we will have to plan for the same well in advance. For example, it would be inappropriate to consider the need to scale up the water-supply and drainage systems in a town after five years, when the population has already reached a threshold. We need to plan and take pragmatic actions today. Civil engineers, who build high-rises in earthquake-prone regions, plan and design earthquake-resistant structures. This is foresight.

Very few people possess this quality. The few who do are able to foresee future possibilities through contemplation. When they act upon our foresight, it paves the way to a life of happiness and splendour. Those who are wise and have exercised their foresight have taken the necessary steps, thereby ensuring their contentment and happiness. Meanwhile, those who lack foresight are flustered by the trials of life and keep complaining about undesirable situations and the unpredictability of life.

We need to act upon the indications we receive through foresight. Thoughts of the future can become a cause for anxiety if we entertain them without purpose. We need not become flustered or worried on account of what we anticipate through foresight. Instead, we simply need to make use of our foresight to improve our present situation. If our present improves, so will our future.

Upfront Investment

The strategy of upfront investment goes hand-in-hand with the gift of foresight. We need to ask ourselves, "What can I change today that will stand me in good stead in the future? What investment can I make today?"

For example, one who is exercising 10 minutes every day, can decide to add two minutes every month to his daily exercise regimen. If he is investing 10 minutes in meditation every day, he will add a minute every week to his meditation session. Even though this additional investment may seem negligible in the beginning, such gradual investments pay great dividends over time. Within six months, the individual will be exercising for around 20 minutes a day, and meditating for over half an hour!

Likewise, we too should contemplate the little actions that we can take up today, which will yield abundant fruit without our conscious attention. Such actions like planting seeds for a future harvest. The little actions we invest today will pay unexpectedly large dividends in the future.

Having discussed some of the key considerations for decision making, we will explore some of the tools that can help in effective decision making in the next chapter.

2

Tools for Effective Decisions

We shall consider some techniques that can help us in making well researched choices.

Impulsive decisions that are made in the head at the spur of the moment, without systematic thinking can be detrimental to us. Therefore, most of the methods that we will discuss now are ways of bringing the situation in writing, and then evaluating the merits and demerits of various options.

Think-it-through technique

When we plan a long-term project or event, it helps to prepare a checklist of its detailed aspects. This process helps reveal loopholes in the choices we make. Breaking the work into smaller units of activities makes the entire project more manageable.

We can then prioritize these small work units to determine the order in which we should tackle each task. This process is called Think-it-through.

During the Think-it-through process, it helps to seek inputs from the people who are involved. It is amazing how every member can bring in a perspective that the remaining team has never thought about. In other words, we can make it a regulated brainstorming session.

Scoring Technique

When we need to make a major decision, we often find ourselves unable to effectively decide the way forward. We are even afraid of making any decision, lest it backfires and turns out to be something that we will regret. We all have many such decisions to make: choosing a course of study and a career path, finding a life partner, deciding where to live, or when to start a family.

When we face a crucial decision, we should be very clear at the outset about why we need to make a choice at a given time. At such junctures, it is quite helpful to weigh the pros and cons of the available options, so as to select the appropriate course of action. Before you move along this course of action, it is important to determine whether it is really going to improve the situation. It may, at times, actually be best to do nothing!

This method consists of two steps :

Step 1: List maximum options.

Consider as many viable options as possible. Very often, the mind gets stuck with a limited number of options that are obvious. We need to look further for more options.

For example, if you are deciding of leaving your job and taking up a new one, you might consider the following options :

1. Move into a new organization;
2. Continue working in the same organization, but choose a different function, department, or role;

3. Change your approach towards your existing role, colleagues and boss;
4. Stay where you are for a certain period, and decide not to decide.

Step 2: Weigh the Pros and Cons.

For each option thus identified, list the pros and cons. Pros are in favour of choosing a given option; cons go against a given option. While listing the pros and cons, consider the impact each option is likely to have on all the aspects of your life - physical, mental, social, financial, and spiritual. For example, if you decide to take a new job out of town, you need to assess the impact this option will have on your family, your financial situation, physical health etc.

Assign a weight to each point and total the scores to determine how the various options line up.

For example, an employee needs to decide whether he should continue his well-paid job in the city or move to a village to teach at the village school. His question is, 'Should I leave this lucrative job and move to the village?' He can list the two options – 'Continue with the job in the city' and 'Move to the village'.

Further, he can list the pros and cons of both options in a table and score them as shown on the next page.

A) Continue with the job in the city

Pros	Cons
More comfortable and convenient lifestyle (+3)	Pollution and stressful lifestyle (-7)
Already own a house here (+5)	Dissatisfaction, not able to do what I love (-5)
Financial strength with substantial income (+4)	Away from the countryside which I love (-3)
Pros → +12	Cons → -15

B) Move to the village

Pros	Cons
Satisfaction of teaching and shaping the next generation (+5)	Will need to settle down and buy a new house (-4)
Can always visit my parents in the city on weekends (+4)	Inconveniences of rural living (-3)
Move from the stressful lifestyle into the more relaxed countryside (+4)	Reduced income (-4)
Pros → +13	Cons → -11

Option A: Continue with the job in the city
The net score for Option A is… +12 − 15 = -3 (a negative score)

Option B: Move to the village and teach in the school

The net score for Option B is… +13 − 11 = +2 (a positive score).

Hence, this individual decides to heed the call of the countryside by casting away the lure of the city job.

The above example was only representative, considering factors at a broad level. In practice, this can be much more elaborate and intricate, considering finer factors that influence the choice.

The Importance-Urgency Matrix

Very often, we struggle with task prioritization. We find it difficult to decide which task should be done first and which task later. The Importance-Urgency matrix helps in tagging tasks based on importance and urgency.

Not everything that is urgent is important. Those who keep reacting to urgent requests may find themselves neglecting what is really important for them. Hence, they need to prioritize their tasks, giving due priority to important tasks, perhaps even over urgent ones.

When we categorize tasks based on their level of importance and urgency, we arrive at four task-lists.

a) Tasks that are important and urgent

Tasks that are both important as well as urgent should be addressed on top priority without delay. These are tasks that you have to own. These are ideally tasks that contribute to our long term goal. They lead to our progress in life. These tasks should ideally not be delegated.

b) Tasks that are important, but not urgent

Such tasks are important with regards to the long term vision for life, but they are not urgent. You can afford to defer such tasks for some time. After noting down such tasks in your diary, the priority should be to designate the time when you plan to work on these tasks. For example, consider your daily exercises. If you are unable to do your exercises in the morning, you can keep it for the evening. Exercise are not urgent; however, they are important to maintain health and vitality.

c) Tasks that are not important, but urgent

These tasks are not important but they are urgent. There are many such tasks that demand immediate attention, although they do not contribute much to the long-term goals of your life.

For example, paying your bills, or booking a train or flight ticket. These are not important, but they have to be time-boxed. You may delegate such tasks to someone and use your time for other important work. If you want to buy something from the market, you can ask someone, who is going to the market, to get it for you. In this way, you can use your time to focus on important tasks.

d) Tasks that are neither important nor urgent

Such tasks are neither important nor urgent. For example, going for a movie, or watching a cricket match. Such tasks need to be given the last preference. These tasks should be dealt with only when you are free from other important or urgent tasks.

Make a list of all your tasks and categorize them into (a), (b), (c), or (d). First find time for the A's, then address the B's, followed by the C's. This will reduce your task-clutter and help you stay in control of your time and workstack. The matrix helps you decide your priorities easily.

Maintain a Faith diary

We make key decisions about how we want to progress in various facets of life, but they are futile as long as they remain in the head. We find that our minds are clouded in everyday situations. We keep vacillating in our heads about what we really want.

We need to take time to write about how we have decided to live each day, and why. When we note down details about what we plan to do, about why we would like to live the way we wish to, we will begin to experience clarity in our decisions. Putting down our thoughts on paper helps us empty the unnecessary mental clutter and create space for new options and choices to emerge.

The Faith diary is a journal that helps you gain clarity about what you really want in life and why. It is like your personal companion, that accompanies you every moment, reminding you about your life choices, your key decisions, the principles that you intend to live by.

You can write details in the Faith diary about how exactly you wish to lead your life. Each one of us has our own unique set of values and aspirations. We do not want to live by others' values. Hence we have to define our own!

Let us look at the benefits of using the Faith diary.

1. Clarity of the goal

Writing down your goal in precise detail increases the probability of getting there faster. When your thoughts are placed carefully on paper with full faith, it serves as a catalyst to aid in their manifestation.

What you write down after contemplation goes deep within your mind. You lend your conscious attention to it. This also helps in arousing positive feelings about the goal. Conscious attention and enthusiasm are pivotal factors in realizing your goal.

Writing down your goals in precise detail is also the most effective way to gain clarity of what you truly want. It directs your attention to what you really want, by de-focusing from what you don't want.

Clearly knowing what you want, why you want it, and when you want it, helps you to evaluate whether you are on track, or when you stray off the life path that you wish to take.

2. Positive programming

By writing the Faith diary, your subconscious mind gets programmed positively. Writing down your goals helps you align your thoughts, feelings, words and actions. It is one way of communicating to nature that you really wish for what you have written.

You get inspired about your goals when you write the Faith diary. This is because your hands, eyes and brain concentrate simultaneously and harmoniously. As a result, the image of what you want is embedded deep within your inner mind, leading to positive results.

3. Saving of time and reinforcement of focus

When your goal is unclear or muddled, your thoughts tend to meander into unproductive channels, thereby dissipating your time and energy. When your goal is clearly laid out before you, you save time. Your energy starts growing in your chosen direction. This also improves your confidence, because the Faith diary imparts firmness to your thoughts and raises your willpower.

Some key points to consider while maintaining a Faith diary:

1. Use a single diary to write about all aspects of your life. Follow a systematic method of writing to avoid irritation later on. Without a systematic method, you will forget where you noted something important and thereby waste time and effort in searching for it or re-writing it. Instead of a diary, you may also use your computer, tablet or mobile phone for efficiently managing your notes.

2. While writing the Faith diary, you must focus only on what you want, not on what you don't want. For example, don't write: 'I don't want illness.' Instead, write: 'I want to enjoy the joy of health.' What you write in your Faith diary will become your reality. Hence, use only positive and inspirational words. Remember that positive words program your subconscious mind positively.

3. Write with faith. It is called the Faith diary, because it is energized by your faith. You are born with incredible power. The need is to awaken the power of faith. The Faith diary will help awaken it. The only requirement is to keep faith!

4. Read with faith. Mere writing is not enough, unless what you have written is reinforced through consistent reading. Read the list of your goals at least three to four times a week. Spend some time reflecting on it. Take a pause to feel what it is like to have achieved the goal. Stay in this feeling of fulfilment for some time.

We have looked at some of the tools that can be used in making decisions easier. In the next chapter, we will discuss the key qualities that are essential to make right decisions.

■

3

Qualities Required for Making Effective Decisions

What differentiates very good decision makers from average or poor decision makers? The quality of our decisions are a product of certain inherent qualities that are put to use. Qualities like good analytical ability, ability to collaborate and communicate, flexibility of the intellect, and sensitivity for subtle details are helpful in making good decisions.

However, there are some subtler foundational qualities that are essential to making effective decisions. Let us consider some of these key qualities.

Resoluteness of Purpose

Those who strive to accomplish their aim in life are the resolute. The first step to be one of the resolute is to decide a goal and be the bearer of an aim. When we become as focused as an archer, who sees nothing else but the target, we become resolute.

There are numerous examples of people who have become resolute. For instance, there are many stories of women who had lost their entire family in accidents, save for their children. Naturally, they were depressed and some even contemplated suicide. But then they looked at their children and were reminded of their responsibility and desire to nurture and bring them up. With an aim defined for them, they were able to overcome their grief.

A definite aim can give meaning and direction to one's life. It also helps to overcome any problem, psychological or otherwise, with ease.

A young stonecutter used to spend hours digging the rocky ground in search of diamonds. The king of the land came across this hardworking man and offered him duties in his court. He gladly accepted. Through hard work, he gradually rose in the ranks to be the chief minister. The former stonecutter led a happy and contended life in the king's court and everyone including the king used to praise him.

On his birthday, the king thought of giving him a fitting gift and decided that the chief minister's portrait be made. He invited all the accomplished artists of the kingdom. "I would like to gift the chief minister with his portrait," he told them. "The one who paints the best picture will be handsomely rewarded." Within a week, all the artists had the minister's portrait ready to be presented to the court. There were paintings which showed the chief minister bedecked in jewels; some showed him holding diplomatic meetings; still others showed him attending to matters under the king's auspices; one portrait even depicted him as the king! Undaunted, the king asked the chief minister, "Which of these is the best?"

To the astonishment of everybody, the chief minister chose the portrait that showed him in torn clothes, muddy and sweating, with a hammer and chisel in his hand. He said, "I had totally forgotten who I was and what I was doing; but this painting has helped me remember my past."

He relinquished the post of chief minister and went back to picking the rocks in search of his treasure.

Life is like that. Unless we are mindful of our aim, we become oblivious to any purpose except for our duties. Have you identified the ultimate aim of your life? If your answer is no, then isn't it about time to zero in on your aim and work towards it as best you can? If you already have an aim, then why not breathe life into it?

With a clear aim, your life has a reason for being and all your decisions would align in that direction. Without a clear aim, trivial problems appear huge and you may feel as if the world is closing in on you at the most trivial inconvenience. You may react to trials and go wrong with your choices.

For those who have not decided their real purpose of life, it is crucial to decide that they will decide their life purpose within a given period. We need to help life to help us. We need not wait for opportunities to come our way, or some king or painter to come our way to remind us of our life purpose! It's likely they will never come.

When you have a powerful aim in your life and walk in that direction, all the forces of nature would rally behind you to propel you in that direction. The aim will act like the rudder of a plane to help you make decisions at various junctures of your life, keeping your aim in focus.

Honesty and Integrity

Honesty and integrity are essential qualities to be able to make the right decisions in life. When people lack honesty, they live with confusion about what they should be doing in situations. What the mind desires to do is not always what ought to be done.

Integrity is a quality that is developed by aligning our thoughts, feelings, speech and actions with our life purpose. Very often, we say what we don't feel, or we don't say what we feel. We don't do what we say, or we do what we actually didn't want to do. This creates a fragmented state of mind, causing our decisions to go wrong.

It is vital that we always remember our life purpose. We must focus our attention towards our goals and not get side tracked by little distractions. Whenever we need to decide something, it always helps to honestly ask ourselves whether our choice will take us towards our goal or away from it.

All of us must choose the option for our highest good instead of choosing a lesser option that might bring us only momentary pleasure. It is often seen that what seems like pleasure in the beginning, turns out to be painful in the long term. What seems painful initially, might be actually progressive in the long term. Our decisions need to reflect this understanding.

Before we decide, we should ask ourselves whether it aligns with our chosen objective in life? If we are able to make this question a habit, the quality of our decisions will improve. When we build our life on the foundation of strong principles, most of our decisions automatically turn out right.

When we have not decided our life principles and values in

detail, then there is bound to be confusion in life. Situations arise, where we are unsure of what to say and what to do. For instance, when a government official is offered bribe for doing a favor, he might refuse it when the stakes are small, say Rs.100 or 1000. But when the stakes are higher, say Rs. 100,000 or a million, he might be caught in two minds about whether to accept the bribe or not. This happens because he has not clearly decided his principles in life.

Deciding the principles and values by which we will lead life makes our lives easy, simple and powerful. In our daily lives, many among us are generally caught up with everyday activities in a way that we seldom find time to introspect and re-think our values, our principles and our goals.

We make key decisions about how we intend to progress in various facets of life, about the kind of life we would love to lead. But the biggest problem is that all this remains a fantasy only in our minds. We do not find enough time to write about what we aspire for, about how we have decided to live each day, and why.

The result of this is stress, disharmony, frustration, health problems, and a general lack of clarity that reflects in our everyday decisions. We don't achieve anything productive when we keep vacillating in our heads about what we really need and why.

However, when we note down the details about what we plan to do, about what our deepest intentions are, and why we would like to live the way we wish to, we will begin to experience a newfound peace and clarity. Writing our thoughts on paper helps us empty the unnecessary mental clutter and creates space for new ideas and new possibilities to emerge. It also helps us align our thoughts with our feelings, our words with our actions, thereby bringing integrity into our life.

Fearlessness

Fear has a debilitating effect on the choices we make. When one is gripped with fear, one's intellectual faculties are not fully available. Many people sense the fear of failure that comes with every new responsibility. Hence, they always stay in their comfort zone and walk the usual beaten path in life.

When we were a child below four years, we used to experiment with something new almost every day. We were never concerned about the outcome. However, the fear-of-outcome has been engrained into the subconscious through the influence of what people around us and the media keep telling us. As grown-ups, many of us have forgotten to experiment with the new. The fear of taking risks tends to stifle our decisions. As a result, we do not explore our fullest potential.

We cannot acquire the treasure in the sea by sitting at the seashore. When we jump into the sea, we automatically learn to swim. And the more we delay this decision of taking the leap, the more we feel frightened of the depths of the sea. Initially we may struggle to stay afloat, but when we eventually learn to swim, it comes naturally and easily to us. Ironically, the water that we feared, itself, helps us stay afloat!

So it is with life. With the fear of failure and calamities, many people remain like bonsais. They may appear to have grown up, but have hardly touched the surface of their real potential.

Those of us, who know swimming, know about this. But do we apply this principle in our lives? Have we learned to cast away the fear of troubled waters in life and take the leap, with the faith that we will eventually learn to swim through the waves of life?

Whenever we have taken up new responsibilities in the past, we may have perhaps experienced fear, struggle and negative thoughts. But with the passage of time, we would have seen how they vanished as we learned to handle the responsibilities. We then focus on fulfilling the responsibility in the best possible way. In truth, we will find that the responsibility lends us energy, just as the water helps us stay afloat.

We also get influenced by social behaviour. When people around us paint a picture of a dangerous world where life is difficult, our belief-system soaks in those fears. The media or people around us may be spreading doubts. Yet, we need not be afraid of new experiments. Courage is the underlying quality for taking bold decisions and calculated risks. If we want make progress in life, we ought to develop courage.

To overcome fear and develop courage, we can adopt the mantra: Face the fear and you will find there is no fear. When fear knocks at your door, let faith opens the door to fear, and you will see that fear vanishes from the scene.

We need to ask ourselves: Do I fear what people will say? Do I have the courage to shoulder the responsibility for my choices? What will I gain by casting away my fears? What am I losing by living in fear? When we get our answers to these questions from within, we will be prepared to take decisions and shoulder responsibilities.

We can adopt the following three steps to overcome fear.

1. Question your fears to discover their fallacy

Most of our fears exist because we are not not prepared to see them straight in the eye. When we face them and observe them in depth, we would invariably find that they did not have any basis. One of the ways of facing our fears is to question ourselves using the law of averages.

Let us understand this with an everyday example. There are people who fear travelling by air due to fear of plane crashes. In such a situation, we can ask ourselves, "Of the thousands of flights that airlines undertake every day, how many actually crash!?" And the answer is: Despite films that depict plane crashes, flying is actually the safest mode of transportation. In fact, the odds of a plane crash are one in a million flights! And the chances of death are 1 in 10 million! On the contrary, road accidents are more common than flying accidents.

Whenever you experience fear, do ask yourself the following three questions. Through these questions, the truth about your fear will be revealed to you.

First question: With whatever I was afraid would occur, have they really occurred?

The answer: No. Only a few events out of those would have occurred.

Second question: With whatever events that did occur, were they as dreadful as I had imagined them to be?

The answer: No. Out of the few that did occur, only a handful were really dreadful.

Third question: However dreadful those countable few events turned out to be, were you able to face them?

Answer: Definitely; I could face them. Life goes on.

If you have faced such events in the past, won't you be able to face such events even in the future? Then why is there a need to fear the future?

You can follow three steps to make decisions despite your worst fears.

Step one: Whenever you are afraid of taking a decision, ask yourself: What is the worst that might happen? Thinking so, prepares you for the worst, whether your worst of fears come true or not. Whatever you think might be the worst, usually does not happen at all. The probability of its occurrence might be barely 5 to 10 percent.

Step two: Accept the worst that can happen. First conjure up what is the worst that could happen. Then accept the worst. If you accept something, then it cannot torment you. Inability to accept something leads to negative feelings.

Step three: Take action in whatever time is left. Without the third step, the first two steps are futile. You know what is the worst that could happen. Hence, in whatever time is left, decide and take relevant action.

By applying this three-step approach you will find that ninety-nine out of hundred times, whatever you feared as the worst, does not occur at all.

2. Become desensitized to your fears

When one does something repeatedly, one becomes desensitized to it. One should do something repeatedly when one fears it. One will find that slowly the fear will vanish.

The skin of our heels get hardened and desensitized by constant contact and friction with hard surfaces like stone, flooring etc. Hence, we do not feel any pain when it rubs against stones or even from the prick of a pin.

In much the same way, if we have the fear of making decisions, or of taking responsibility, or of completing a task, then we should face them repeatedly. Whenever we get the opportunity to drive away the fear, we should use that opportunity. This way, we become desensitized to the feeling of fear.

3. Learn to laugh at your fears

We need to learn to laugh at our fears. Laughter acts like a medicine. Few are those, who can laugh at their fears. When you laugh at your fears, it reduces the intensity of the fear.

It's easy to smile when things are going our way. However, it is a sign of courage if we can laugh heartily when nothing seems to be going our way. It is easy to laugh at others, but it requires a mature mind to be able to laugh at oneself.

It helps to decide that whenever we feel afraid of taking any decision or responsibility, we shall first smile at the situation. This will act as a medicine to drive away the fear and open up our intellectual faculties to decide effectively.

There have been so many revolutionary creations that did not see the light of the day just only because people chose to succumb to their fears. They were overly concerned about what people would say if they failed, or they just didn't have faith in their own potential.

Faith

When one lacks conviction that they would be able to make something happen, they stop even before they start on the project. There can always be difficulties to start with something new. People may not support you; or they may even speak against your ideas. This initial hurdle has to be surmounted. And this is where faith and confidence play an important role in decision making.

You are blessed with the ultimate solution that can surmount any difficulties in life - Faith. Nature makes this arrangement within you much before you are put to test with challenges in life.

Faith is at the core of our existence. Faith is the most potent power given to you, that is waiting to be expressed to its fullest. It is only when we express the quality of faith that we get a sense of accomplishment and contentment. Everyone possesses faith. It's just that it is expressed in varied degrees in various people.

Faith is the foundation of success in all human endeavour. Without faith, we can easily fall a prey to the doubts and negative beliefs of the mind. Every human being who lacks faith is a slave to the mind and is tormented by it. When faith awakens, one becomes the master of the mind.

Faith is to believe what you do not see; the reward of this faith is to get to see what you believe. By stifling this latent quality of faith, man leads a very limited life. Without faith, life is infested with doubts and false assumptions. Faith crumbles in the presence of doubts and is eventually replaced by fear. A fearful person leads a constricted and painful life. One who has faith lives freely and happily. They can make decisions with an open mindset without any doubts or conflicts within.

When we attain what we want through the power of faith, we develop conviction and confidence. As soon as our confidence manifests to the fullest, miracles begin to occur in our lives. Nature works according to certain principles. When faith and confidence are kindled within us, then according to the ways of nature, miracles are bound to occur.

We need to recognize and awaken the faith that is hidden within us, instead of waiting for favourable events to raise our faith.

It is a law of nature that we get evidences of whatever we believe in. You may have heard the famous maxim, 'Seeing is believing'. The truth is actually the reverse: 'Believing is seeing'. When we understand this secret; we will realize that our reality can be shaped by our faith in whatever we choose to believe. When we have faith, it shows up in the decisions we take.

Discernment of the right value

Discerning the right value for anything – be it something that attracts us, or an incident that shakes us up – is a key quality for making higher choices in life.

Imagine that you are visiting a shop to buy a matchbox. The shopkeeper is selling the matchbox for ten rupees. And the neighbouring shopkeeper is selling similar matchboxes for five rupees each. Would you then buy the one that is priced at ten rupees? You won't. The neighbouring shopkeeper is selling it at five rupees. This implies that ten rupees is overpriced for this matchbox.

What if the shopkeeper changes his mind and is prepared to sell it at eight rupees? Would you still buy it? No, you won't, because you now know the right price for the matchbox. You know its right value. You won't settle for anything more than its right value.

Let us draw parallels from the matchbox value to the incidents in our lives. We know very well what the right value is for a matchbox, but do we do the same for incidents or situations in our lives?

There are so many incidents that occur in our lives, where we get gripped by anger, or fear, or contempt. There would have been incidents or situations where we had to make up our minds and respond appropriately. We may have over-reacted or escaped these situations by giving them exaggerated value. As a result, we may have chosen the wrong response in those situations, leading to further problems.

What value ought to be given to certain incidents, and what value are you giving them? In every incident or situation, first decide how much it is worth. How much time, attention, or energy would you afford to spend on it? And when you decide the value, give it only that much.

The interesting aspect is that each one has their own value for a given thing. And this depends on their aim in life and their level of maturity. The trouble is that we get swayed by the value that others would generally give to a particular incident and then imitate them. We need to first consider what our aim in life is. What is the understanding that we have gained in life? We can then value a given thing based on such careful reflection.

For example, someone who is attending a job interview feels shaken by some discouraging remarks from the panel of interviewers. He feels demoralized and enraged, and decides to walk out. If he would remember the purpose of his being there in the interview, he would decide not to give as much value to those remarks and get through with the interview with patience and poise.

Using the above example of the matchbox, a good question that we can always ask ourselves is: What is the matchbox value for this incident (or thing, or situation)? This will remind us to weigh the situation in the light of our goals and give it only as much time or energy as we can afford.

■

4

Collective Decision Making in a Group

Decision making can seem even more complex when it requires the integration of diverse views in a group – whether it be a family or an organization of people.

Decisions that we take in a group may not necessarily align with the personal opinions of some of the members of the group. They may either feel let down or that their views have not been considered. Each person thinks differently, and hence arriving at a collective decision becomes all the more challenging.

Diverse views, Common Vision

When there are a variety of views and opinions, they can be harnessed for innovation. Even in a household, the different views of the wife, husband, and children can be combined in the decision making process, provided they have the same vision for the family. The constructive product of different viewpoints can bring forth an altogether new dimension.

Not all fingers of the hand are of same length. Evolution has designed our hands to be as versatile as possible. The different lengths of fingers have been tailored by nature to perform all tasks adequately – whether it is to operate a pen, a computer mouse, kitchen tools, or to smash a block of wood. If all the fingers were of the same length, it would be impossible to perform many tasks like gripping or climbing. Thus the difference in the fingers is a blessing.

Similarly, each person has a different nature, a different viewpoint, and a unique thought process. Yet, each can contribute towards a common vision. Having a variety of perspectives is actually a strength that can be leveraged for making decisions in a common direction.

Every member of a group, needs to value the importance of diversity of perspectives. Diverse viewpoints, when channelized in a systematic manner, can contribute to the team vision.

People can be classified into two categories based on their mental faculties. Those with left-brain predominance are logical and methodical in their thought processes. Those with right-brain predominance are creative, intuitive, and can work wonders with colours and pictures, though their thought processes may appear illogical.

Nothing in this world is useless. Even the most illogical perspective can actually serve as a bridge towards growth. If both these categories of people exist within a group, it can be a blessing if their strengths can be identified and leveraged harmoniously. Decisions that bring the strengths of both these perspectives can work wonders. When both these kinds of people work together constructively, then the result will be that of a Bright-brain that can bring forth innovative ideas and execute them.

Become comfortable and skillful at creative conflict

While taking decisions in a group, many of us feel like avoiding conflict. The fear and discomfort that come with conflict is understandable, as some conflicts have been known to hurt people. However, the idea that conflict is negative is often a limiting belief. This limiting belief sets us up to miss opportunities to take advantage of the creative forces of conflict. To reap the fullest benefits from conflict, we have to change how we think about it.

Conflict is a force filled with tension and energy. We can learn to leverage conflict creatively to open the door to new possibilities. Conflict invites us to arrive at innovative decisions or to gain important insights into ourselves. Conflict is inevitable when the group empowers members who have diverse views. If no one cares to argue for their views, the energy to develop a common vision for the group will be missing.

Innovative decisions are made collectively in a group when there is creative energy, when the status quo is challenged by a desire for something new. To be able to effect changes, we need to incorporate multiple perspectives to broaden our ideas. We have a greater chance of success when we include stakeholders who don't see things our way. Hence, it helps to welcome opposing opinions into discussions.

In order to leverage conflicts creatively, we need to learn to be comfortable and skillful at managing conflicts. When we view situations subjectively and personally, our perspective gets muddled up and we falter with our decisions. We need to acquire emotional intelligence and learn to separate people from processes and issues.

This does not mean that there aren't risks when dealing with differences. We can learn to anticipate those risks and learn the attitudes and skills needed to channel creative conflict, so that it works for us rather than against us.

Reiterate the group vision

A clear and compelling vision is the best way to engage and empower the group. It unleashes their performance in unimaginable ways when the vision is often repeated and described with passion.

A truly compelling vision is a joy to share. If leaders do not repeat their group's vision often, it could be a sign that the vision is not truly inspiring. Amidst all the noise, repetition helps something as important as the group's vision to sink in. It helps in aligning divergent perspectives within the team toward the common vision.

Acquiring consent from others

Acquiring the cooperation of people around you is paramount to achieve success in various facets of life. Some people have the habit of frequently getting into debates and conflicts. They do not realize that this tendency makes it difficult for them to secure the support of people to achieve their objective.

People find the easy way of criticizing others to assert their superiority. They feel elated by looking down upon others. Hence, they tend to seek opportunities to criticize others. This tendency only creates foes of potential friends.

Instead of criticizing, we need to develop the art of 'criti-guiding'. Before telling people about their weaknesses or areas of improvement, we can first genuinely tell them about their virtues and then convey their potential areas of improvement in a positive tone, without hurting them. This way, people will come to regard you as their well-wisher and receive your feedback positively.

Some people find it difficult to get concurrence from colleagues or family on matters pertaining to their professional or personal decisions. They are unable to convince people that their decision is right for them. It is not practically possible to always get people's agreement on our views. People have diverse viewpoints based on their backgrounds. Though they may not necessarily agree with you, it is still possible to get their concurrence.

A key reason why people do not take decisions is their desire that all the concerned people should agree to their decision. When they do not get approval from certain people, people feel let down and back out. The art of making decisions in such circumstances requires you to work through the disagreements peacefully and with a sense of genuine goodwill.

We can find a middle path through conflicts by acquiring concurrence on some aspects, if not all. This requires skilful communication, healthy human relations and an understanding of human psychology. Each person has certain psychological needs. How do people stand to benefit by cooperating with us? Which of their needs would be fulfilled? If we understand their needs and address them even partly, if not fully, then they will be prepared to cooperate.

We need to step into their shoes to understand how they can cooperate. If we do not connect at a deeper level with them and merely demand their cooperation at a superficial level, they may perhaps turn it down on us. Are they going to be benefitted emotionally, physically or financially? Is it their duty and responsibility to cooperate? What good does our approach do to their self-image?

When we understand the psychological needs of people, we can communicate with them accordingly. They need to realize that they are helping themselves by cooperating. When we look at things from the others' point of view, it helps us communicate with them in an amenable way.

Before communicating with people and seeking their agreement, it helps to speak about those points which they already agree upon. For example, before seeking their agreement, it can be discussed and agreed that we all desire that the work should be completed on time and in the best possible manner. When everybody desires this, then you have won half the battle of winning their agreement. Those points on which there is already a common agreement should be discussed first. We can then settle for a partial agreement on matters where there is conflict of opinions.

Nations need people who can participate in international negotiations and strike agreements, because they know that art. Many organizations also have people whose job is to dialogue with other parties, customers etc. and create a genuine feeling of a win-win to acquire their agreement.

Companies do not appoint people, who lose their temper during discussions across the table. Most often, people may say something, but the real reason behind their disagreement could be something different. People tend to be self-centred when they are faced with conflicts. They overlook the interests of others who are involved and narrow their focus on their own interests. It is essential that they understand the genuine underlying problems that others might be facing in cooperating. They can then empathize, appreciate and address those concerns to seek their cooperation for mutual benefit.

The one who learns this art has the knack of understanding the real reasons why people do not cooperate. They can get things done effectively by smoothly sailing through conflicts.

In the chapters that follow, we shall delve deeper into the our internal state of being, which is the ultimate influencer for all our decisions. We will consider how we can hone the power of intuition in the next chapter.

∎

5

Guidance through Intuition

When we have an important decision to make, many of us tend to search outside for answers. We seek guidance from our family or friends. We even read literature or guidelines offered by those who are well known and proficient. These days, we even Google for solutions! However, we often neglect the most reliable source of all – the Source within us.

The Source of all answers

As a human being, we are constantly in one of three states: waking, dreaming, or deep (dreamless) sleep. In the waking state, we perceive the world through our senses – sights through the eyes, sounds through the ears, smells and tastes through the nose and tongue, touch through the skin.

However, the world that we perceive as our reality is only a partial reality. The risk of being limited to this partial reality is that we begin to judge and assume the complete reality on the basis of whatever we perceive through our senses.

The truth is that our sense perceptions are interpreted by the mind to make up a derived reality. Our reasoning is therefore based on this partial reality that we perceive through our senses and the mind. This limits our decision making. Decisions can arise from the source of boundless wisdom when we go beyond the limits of the mind and access its source.

What is the source of the mind? From where do thoughts emerge? When we experience the source of the mind, the complete reality is revealed. The Source (consciousness) is the living essence that exists beyond the mind, beyond the states of waking, dream and deep sleep.

The Source is beyond the concepts of time and space. It is a state of wholeness beyond duality. The nature of consciousness is 'knowing', which is beyond 'thinking'. Knowing comes first, thinking comes later. Hence, consciousness precedes thoughts. For this reason, it is the source of boundless intelligence. And it is the source of all answers!

As it is beyond the realm of finite thoughts, the Source is not subject to the limited constructs and confines of rational thinking. Hence, it is the ocean of inspiration and intuition.

The Heart – the seat of the Source

You have heard people say, "This is from my heart", "I wrote from my heart", "All my compositions simply flow from my heart", "I am going with the flow", and so on. What are they referring to? They are referring to an inner experience which comes from the seat of 'Being', which is beyond the knowledge of the mind.

This experience is beyond the language of the mind. When it is being experienced, the ideas, choices, and creations that emerge will make you wonder about their expression – "How did such an idea come about? Such ideas never emerged before!"

When a poet composes an exquisite piece of poetry, he himself is amazed. He wonders, 'How did such poetry emerge from within me!' The poet knows the words but not how to combine and compose them. As soon as he moves away from the clamor of thoughts, as soon as he transcends his mind and reaches the heart, such compositions begin to emerge by inspiration.

We have seen how consciousness is the very essence of our knowingness beyond thoughts. But then, where does consciousness connect with the human body? It can be said to be roughly in the area of the heart. However, this is not the physical heart. It is the subtle place where the formless reality unites with the physical form. It can be called the subtle place, because it is not a location that can be physically pointed out. It is the seat of inner experience, the seat of the Source. It can be *felt* as the area around the heart.

When you reach the seat of your Being, you access your original state. This state is like a gateway into the 'now'. 'Now' is where there is neither yesterday nor tomorrow. It is the gateway to liberation from the impressions of the past and the anxieties or imaginations of the future. It is liberation from misery. It is not in the head, but in the heart.

By being present in this experience of Being in the heart and operating from there, you are helping your heart to take over your life. Whenever you have to make a decision, dive within and consult your heart. You shall receive guidance from within; directly from the source, from consciousness – the all-knowing principle that permeates the universe.

We need to learn the art of connecting to the Source of all answers. Whenever we are faced with any problem or want to decide something, we can close our eyes and shift to the heart. The message you are sending to the universe is that you are ready and willing to receive guidance. Guidance will then automatically flow from the heart.

Developing the Power of Intuition

Great creations are possible when we are rooted in the experience of the Source. This is because the Source expresses through bodies that are receptive, and through which innovations can be manifested. All creative processes are enlivened by pure consciousness and directed by its intelligence.

This vast intelligence can be accessed by developing the power of intuition. Intuition is the ability to connect with the Source within us and receive guidance. In other words, intuition is in-tuition – receiving tuition from within.

We all have invariably experienced the spark of intuition sometime in our lives. For example, have you ever experienced that you are thinking of someone and the phone rings and that person is on the line?

This is a very common example of intuition at work. Our intuition is a faculty that can be strengthened and put to effective use to make the best choices; to take the best decisions for our lives.

Intuition is present within everyone. It is just that some are more attuned to it, while others rarely pay heed to it. The common question that many people ask is how the power of intuition can be developed. Here are some steps on how to develop your intuition and use it to take more effective decisions in your life.

1. Recognize when the Source communicates

The Source showers its benevolence upon us, providing us with hints which, if grasped properly, can propel us in the right direction.

To be able to use your intuition and attune with the Source, it is essential to recognize when it speaks to you. Communication from the heart does not often come in clear words or sentences. It can come in the subtlest ways through feelings or fleeting ideas.

The Source has its own language for communicating with us. They may be visual messages, through a written signboard or book that we stumble upon. They might be auditory, through striking statements we happen to hear; or intuitive messages communicated through our feelings. It calls out to us through these means as if to say, "Look here, focus on this aspect."

For example, you may receive impressions in the form of images that appear in quick flashes. It can be a hunch or a particular word. If you are unable to grasp what is being intuited, you may even enter into a dialogue by asking questions and requesting clear indications to get more information and clarity. Your intuition can also communicate through physical sensations such as a feeling of discomfort in your stomach, or goosebumps, or a feeling of relief.

You may receive intuitive messages through emotions, such as uneasy feeling when the intuition is steering you away from something, or profound peace, certainty and ease when you're being guided along a path that will lead you to happiness and wellbeing.

Sometimes your intuition communicates through a deep sense of knowing and certainty. There may have been times when you have felt that you knew something to be true deep within; it is likely that it is your intuition communicating.

Intuition is not a one-way process. It can be a dialogue, where you actively converse with the Source by being in the heart. You ask for guidance.

2. Ask for specific guidance

While you open yourself to guidance from the Source, it is also possible to ask for specific guidance. This is what prayer is all about. The more clearly you present your questions to the Source within, the clearer the guidance.

And when we ask through prayer, it is not enough. We need to be be receptive for answers that come from within. This is where the practice of meditation comes in.

3. Practice meditation regularly

If prayer is the question, then meditation is the answer. Prayer is only half the magic. Meditation completes the magic. People focus on prayer, on visualization and other techniques to impress upon their subconscious mind. But they miss the all-important need to meditate.

You ask for something through prayer. But then you have to be in silence to receive the answer. In other words, being in meditation makes you receptive and attuned to the creative principle, so as to receive what you have prayed for.

When you place an order in the restaurant, you cannot keep calling the bearer repeatedly. You need to give him time to go and fetch your order. In the same way, if you keep ruminating in thoughts, you are not allowing the wondrous gift of prayer to work for you. When you bring a much-needed pause through the practice of meditation, it creates the space in which what you have prayed for, can be manifested in your life.

The Source is teeming with boundless wisdom, only waiting for us to be receptive, so that it can spring forth with the most wondrous ideas. To become more receptive to the Source, you need to connect deeply with it. Abiding in the silence of the heart, you will become more sensitive to subtle impulses that arise within.

Practicing meditation regularly will help you detach from the constant noise of thoughts in the head and shift to the serenity of the heart. Even spending 10 to 15 minutes consistently at the same time every day can deepen your attunement with the heart and raise your ability to recognize when your intuition speaks.

4. Write down your answers

Messages arising from intuition are subtle and can fade out of your awareness within seconds. Hence, it helps to write down the insights that arise as quickly as possible, lest they are lost.

The Source expresses its wisdom through minds that are receptive to inspiration from the heart. Hence, when you write down these flashes of insight, you are indicating to nature that you are open to receive and serious about acting on them.

You can maintain a journal for recording your intuitions for ten minutes daily. This practice is a way of strengthening the power of your intuition. When this is consistently practiced, you will marvel at the clarity of what comes through from the heart.

Your decisions will arise from the place of boundless wisdom, which cannot be matched by any level of analytical reasoning.

5. Let the heart choose to use the head

Acquiring guidance from the heart does not mean that we should not use analytical reasoning. The intellect is a tool that can be used to plan effectively and evaluate alternatives and outcomes.

However, when should the intellect be used? For most people, the thoughts in the head takeover their lives. Their attention is invested in their thoughts to such an extent that they rarely dip into the heart and seek guidance.

When you hone your power of intuition, you learn to abide in the heart and allow your life to be directed from the Source This means that the intellect, or the reasoning mind can be effectively used, provided it is directed from the heart. When the heart suggests the use of the intellect, then we can use it by all means.

The other by-product of relying on the thoughts in the head is that the personalized ego takes credit for innovative ideas that arise from the heart. This limits the flow of ideas, as the ego draws boundaries and personalizes everything.

When we understand that the body and mind can be an effective medium for the most creative and phenomenal ideas to be manifested from the Source of everything, we will begin to live in receptive gratitude for how the Source guides our lives.

6. Recognize the inner voice by noting telltale signs

How do we become more familiar with the voice of intuition

within us? Besides following all the steps mentioned earlier, we also need to note telltale signs that act as signposts.

Suppose that you are meeting a stranger and he appears very convincing and trustworthy. However, you go by your gut feel and decide not to deal with him. You then meet your friend and discuss about the stranger. Your friend says, "You're in luck that you didn't proceed with him. I know people who have complained about his integrity."

Now, your gut-feel was actually sounding warning bells. The consequences prove that your inner voice was guiding you. When this is so, you should try to recall and reflect on how exactly you were feeling when you were conversing with the person. What were the body sensations that you felt? Was it a heaviness or uneasiness in the stomach? Or a sore sensation in the chest? Or was it just an unexplainable feeling of discomfort or an unknown fear?

Note these telltale signs in your journal. Verify them across many such occurrences. With this, you can refine your sensitivity to the inner voice, as you would be learning its language.

7. Take prompt action

When you act sincerely and promptly on the guidance you receive from the Source within, you receive even more guidance that is specific and easier to decipher. Faith is the key to action. When you trust your intuition and act, you begin to harmonize and synchronize your life with the higher guidance.

Whether you want to make better decisions or solve problems effectively, you will rely on your intuition to guide you. The more you see the miraculous working of your intuition, the more you will trust it and act upon it.

Trusting your intuition is about trusting life itself. It is about trusting what your true essence intends in this life. Even if the guidance is at odds with the chatter of thoughts in the head, it is faith in the divine perfection of the Source that will stand you in good stead in making the right decisions. The next chapter delves deeper into this.

■

6

Decisions from Higher Consciousness

Ultimate success in life is attained when decisions arise from higher consciousness. In the earlier chapter, we have discussed about the Source of all answers that is available in the heart.

We will now go deeper into the essence of consciousness and the body-mind mechanism, so as to understand how we can recognize and abide in higher consciousness and allow decisions to happen from that standpoint.

Consciousness is the living, sentient principle due to which the body is alive. It is only owing to the presence of consciousness—the knowing principle—that our eyes can see; it is only due to its presence that thoughts arise.

The human body is non-sentient. it is non-living from its very birth. It is only in the presence of consciousness that our otherwise non-sentient body springs into life. Knowing happens through the medium of the body. Thus, it is not the body that knows; the body cannot know. It is consciousness that is knowing through the medium of the body-mind mechanism.

The Experience of Being

Thoughts ceaselessly arise and subside in the light of awareness. However, thoughts have nothing to do with the awareness of being alive. This experience is beyond thoughts. Thinking has nothing to do with Being. We can consider the experience of Being as the screen on which the movie of thoughts is being projected.

The mind tries to understand it by imagining it. Rene Descartes, a 17th century French philosopher once said, "I think, therefore I am." However, if existence were dependent on thinking, then we wouldn't exist if we stopped thinking. This is certainly not the case. When we are in deep sleep, we don't think but we continue to exist. We even comment on waking that we had sound sleep. We have to exist during deep sleep to be able to know that we did sleep well.

Being comes first, thinking comes later. Being (Awareness) is our essential nature. It is who we truly are. It is the most obvious truth about us. Yet, it is lost in the constant chatter of thoughts. Thinking cannot lead to the experience of Being. To experience Being, we need to clearly watch what *is*.

When the judging and reasoning mind is made still, the experience of conscious presence is revealed. In that state, there's no need to think about it. Presence is independent of thought. Presence just *is*. It is the most obvious experience, the open secret – so open and obvious that we easily fail to notice it. A clear glimpse of our true nature can awaken us from our limiting beliefs about who we are and shift us onto this enlivening presence which we truly are.

The song of presence is playing constantly; you *are* that song. Abiding in this presence is the experience of pure joy, unconditional and boundless, independent of the world, untouched by situations.

We have been programmed to believe that we are our limited body-mind. Due to this limiting belief, we attempt to gain success or happiness through whatever we do. And we continue believing this without doubt because we see everyone else around us in the same pursuit.

Ultimate success is attained when we abide in the experience of pure awareness, pure presence beyond the mind and body. This is the seat of infinite wisdom. Being in this experience, decisions need not be deliberated; they arise naturally as inspiration from the seat of wisdom.

Perceiving situations from Pure Awareness

The stream of thoughts continually passes in our awareness. This is like the advertisement ticker that keeps scrolling in the strip below the TV news bulletin. When we abide in pure awareness, we allow the thread of thoughts to keep flowing, while remaining focussed on the main news which is the 'I AM' – the sense of conscious presence. This makes it possible to detach from thoughts and allow consciousness to shape our life.

This does not mean that we are escaping or not paying heed to the situations that life throws up. Abiding in pure awareness does not amount to escaping from situations. On the contrary, being in pure awareness is the only true way of addressing situations. By resting in awareness, we need not solve problems. Rather, we will witness solutions arising from the problem situation itself!

The need for a solution is an imagined need that arises from the working of the mind. In a dark room, if you mistake a rope to be a snake, then you will start searching for a stick to hit the snake. What you really need is a torch, which will show you the fallacy of the snake. It will make you see the rope as a rope. In the same way, the need for finding a solution arises at the mental level due to a clouded perception of the situation.

When we are away from our true nature of pure awareness, the mind tends to give situations and events undue importance by resisting them. Seeing the situation as a problem is the only problem. When we look at situations through the lens of our limiting beliefs, we resist them. Resistance causes the situations to persist. It causes confusion and indecision.

Problems that occur at a given level of awareness can never be solved at the same level of awareness. We need to raise our awareness to be able to witness clearly. With pure witnessing from a higher awareness, the problem no longer remains a problem. We begin to notice our beliefs and notions that are distorting our view, causing us to see the situation as a problem.

By abiding in pure awareness, we allow the so-called problem to settle in the space of acceptance. We no longer resist it. We don't get into a discord. We flow in joyous harmony with whatever is happening. We remain aware of whatever *is*, without attaching any special meaning to it.

When we lend our detached presence through this way of pure being, the solution emerges from the so-called problem situation itself. If the solution demands action, you will then witness all the necessary actions *happening* through you or whoever else participates in the scene.

This is the highest way of decision-making. It is the ultimate way to solve problems, because we don't need to solve anything – we see it 'dissolving'! Higher awareness is the solution in itself.

We need to experience how solutions unfold from the situations when you abide in pure awareness. This will help develop conviction in our true nature and faith in this highest approach to decision-making.

The art of abiding in pure awareness

We need to learn the art of connecting with pure awareness and abiding therein. Whenever we are faced with any problem or want to decide something, we should close our eyes and shift to pure awareness.

In order to remain rooted in the center, in pure awareness, you need to constantly keep a check on any drift of attention towards the content of thoughts. One, who is always alert, alone can remain at the center. One, who is not aware, tends to gravitate towards the world of myriad thoughts and remains stuck there. The drift away from the heart towards the realm of thoughts makes us lose our awareness.

When we are lost to our true essence, even the simplest tasks may appear difficult in the web of our thoughts. We hold onto thoughts and get lost in the chain of thoughts that follow. But no sooner do we let go of our thoughts, we find ourselves at our center, in pure awareness.

Holding onto anything amounts to 'doing' and requires effort. On the other hand, letting go of everything leads to 'being', which is effortless. Here, nothing needs to be *done* to let go. Nothing could be easier than being in pure awareness. Even breathing or blinking one's eyes is 'doing' which requires effort as against effortless 'being'.

Suppose you are standing in front of the mirror, lost in your thoughts. Even though your face is visible in the mirror, when you are preoccupied with your thoughts, you aren't really seeing your face. It is easy to come out of your train of thoughts if someone just waves a hand in front of you.

In the same way, we tend to get lost in the imaginations of the mind and do not return to reality. Even though returning to reality or awareness is the easiest thing of all, it *appears* difficult to the mind. The utter simplicity of just 'being' is difficult for the mind as anything the mind can conceive or imagine is far more complex and farfetched.

We get enamored by the content of our thoughts so easily that we are unaware of how our attention is invested in it. Even within the world of thoughts, we classify thoughts as good or bad, positive or negative, worthy or worthless, depending on our beliefs.

In the Indian epic, the Mahabharata, when the war was about to begin, Lord Krishna led Arjuna to the center of the battlefield, from where he had an even view of both the sides that were about to war. He advised Arjuna to go beyond both – his attachment to what he considered good and also his aversion to what he considered bad. Lord Krishna directed Arjuna to watch the impending war from the standpoint of higher awareness, without being pulled into any form of bias.

This holds a key symbolic message for us. We need to rise above our perceptions of good and bad, beyond the pairs of opposites that exist in our thoughts, and view the situation from the standpoint of pure awareness.

Further, Lord Krishna directed Arjuna to let go of his personal egocentric desires and be established in the Source (God), serving as a medium for divine expression of the Source. This implies the need to shift from ego-centered decisions that arise from the personalized mind and rest in the bliss of the true Self – pure consciousness. Being established in pure consciousness, the body and mind will serve to enact the decisions that arise from our true essence.

One who seeks guidance from the heart by abiding in pure awareness is open to inspiration. He alone can make the most appropriate choices and solve problems in a complete way. Today, the world needs leaders who are guided from the heart.

Deciding from higher consciousness

Decisions that arise from higher consciousness are right, even though they may externally appear inappropriate. At the same time, decisions that arise from the mental noise in the head are bound to be wrong, even though they may externally seem to be perfect. Before deciding on any action, one should first raise one's level of consciousness. Then the decision will be right.

Zen masters in Japan used to teach self-defence techniques like Kung Fu, Judo or Karate to their disciples. The disciples used to fight using these techniques. The real purpose of training in these arts was not to fight, but rather to practice living from higher consciousness.

The fighters were called Samurais. When two Samurais would fight, their primary aim was retain their level of consciousness without letting it fall during the fight. The real war was to maintain peace within!

Once, two Samurais were engaged in a duel. When one of the Samurais was on the verge of winning, the other Samurai spat on his face. The one who was winning immediately withdrew and stopped fighting, accepting defeat. When he was asked why he stopped fighting when he was just on the verge of victory, his answer is one that is worth contemplating on.

He said, "When my opponent spat on me, a strong emotion of hatred arose within me. I felt that it was not right to fight any further with this lowered state of awareness." He remembered his master's teaching: "Whatever you do with lowered consciousness will be wrong. The outward action may seem to be right, but the feeling behind it is important. You should not fight with anybody when filled with hatred."

During the fight, there should be a spirit of sportsmanship. Otherwise, people show hatred towards their opponents, which gives rise to bitterness, anger and hatred between players. The sporting atmosphere of the game is spoilt.

Hence, outward action may appear right, but we should ask ourselves what our inner feelings are. If we take any action from lowered consciousness, it is bound to go wrong or backfire in the future. Those, who do not understand this, take decisions impulsively under the influence of negative feelings. Very often, decisions are driven by the need to safeguard one's sense of security under the pretext of some excuse. Hence, our decisions ought to be taken from higher awareness.

A young gynaecologist, who has begun his practice, wants to be successful in his career and earn a good sum of money so that he can establish his own hospital. There is nothing wrong with this intention. But now, if a patient approaches this doctor for abortion, what should he do?

The mind looks for fixed answers. It demands: "Tell me clearly, should I do this, or shouldn't I?" The limited intellect does not think beyond 'Yes' and 'No'. When one sees this situation from higher consciousness, one will understand that the decision depends upon the situation in hand.

The doctor has to weigh whether the abortion will help the mother. If the abortion is not done, could it be fatal for the mother? What is the condition of the foetus? What will be the condition if the child is born? He should also see whether the patient or her family has wrong intentions in aborting the child. What would be the effect of the abortion on the patient's family? His decision will change, depending on the situation. You can see that the decision cannot be just 'Yes' or 'No'. Decisions should be taken by considering all aspects. In every situation, think about new options out-of-the-box.

A general compassionate consideration that naturally arises from higher consciousness is to benefit as many people as possible. Decisions should be in the common interest of the masses, rather than favouring just a few. This is one of the important considerations of a higher choice.

■

7

Making the Highest Choice

Our everyday choices determine our future. Since our choices shape our future, we need to ask ourselves: What are the choices that we are making today? How is our future shaping up?

Each and every choice we make has an effect on our lives. Hence, we need to learn the art of consistently making the highest choice. This art will prove to be a blessing in the future. If we have mastered the technique of consistently giving a *comprehensive response* in various situations in life, then we can make the highest choice at every juncture in life.

To understand what a comprehensive response means, let us first look at the various kinds of responses that we give in our daily lives.

1. Prompt response: This is a quick response. For example, you give a quick response when you want to get up early in the morning. You get out of bed as soon as the alarm goes off.

2. Aggressive response: A prompt response can change into an aggressive response when you are impatient or angry or when somebody hurts your ego. Such a response has to be avoided.

3. Polite or Patient response: This type of response is required to bring peace in situations or to avoid heated arguments.

4. Opposite response: An opposite response is when you give a response that is exactly contrary to what could be anticipated. An opposite response does not mean giving an inappropriate or wrong response. An opposite response is a response that dispels disappointments, laziness, and anger from life. On the other hand, it is an invitation to hope, creativity, and happiness.

   For example, when we are faced with defeat due to some reason, we can choose to give an opposite response by not considering it as our defeat. We can treat the defeat as a stepping stone to learn lessons from our mistakes and take the flight to success.

5. Comprehensive response: The same type of response need not work in all situations. We should be able to clearly identify and apply the various types of responses in relevant life situations. Where you need to give a prompt response, you will do just that. Where you need to give a humble response, you will give a humble response. Where a patient response is required, you will choose to wait; and where an opposite response is the need of the hour, you will go ahead with that.

   If you can give all these responses appropriately in relevant situations, then it means that you have learnt to give a comprehensive response.

What is the highest choice?

Whatever situation we find ourselves in, whatever activity we are engaged in, we should always question ourselves, 'Am I making the highest choice for this given moment?'

If a student, who has decided to devote time to his studies during a given period, instead wastes time in useless gossip, then he has not made the highest choice. Spending time in gossip also lends shape to your future. If the student fails in the exams, or does not score well, he may complain, "I never desired this outcome. I wanted to pass the exams with good scores, the questions in the exam were too difficult."

People are unaware that their choices are shaping their future, and so they continue to make choices in everyday life without careful contemplation. As a result, when they stumble upon an undesired future created by their own choices, they grumble, "We never anticipated this."

We should clearly recognize that our future is the result of our own choices. Reading this book at this given moment, for example, could be your highest choice for this moment. You could have made many other choices like spending time watching TV, or indulging in hobbies indiscriminately. But you have made the highest choice of reading this book now. This choice can likely pave the way to a better future.

Very often, one may actually feel happy for the given moment in making a particular choice, but it is possible that it may lead to an unfavourable future. The need is to raise the level of awareness and remain vigilant when a choice is to be made. If we are able to do so successfully, then we can consciously shape our future as we desire.

The art of making the highest choice

In order to be able to make the highest choice consistently, you need to make up your mind about what you wish to create in life. What is it that you are actually aspiring for in and through all your pursuits? Once you have made up your mind, you can then constantly observe yourself diligently and ask yourself at every juncture: Am I making the highest choice as per my chosen life purpose?

When we are not clear about our life purpose, we tend to deviate in many other directions by entertaining aspirations that contradict one another. As a result, we ordain a mixed future of contradictions, which confuse us even further.

For example, suppose that an engineer dreams of working on research projects in the labs of NASA. At the same time, if he does not wish to leave his hometown to fulfil this dream, then these are mutually contradictory aspirations. As a result, he would waste a significant period, making inappropriate choices. The result will be confusion and dilemma.

Therefore, it is essential to have clarity about one's purpose of life and to carefully work out the smaller aims that can lead to the attainment of the larger life purpose.

If an person does not like his job, his mind may find numerous excuses to avoid work. The mind fools itself with such excuses. Choosing to dwell in such excuses and avoiding work will lend shape to an undesirable future.

First, we need to be alert about the choice that we are making every moment. When do we falter with our choices? When are our choices mediocre? And when do we make higher choices?

To recognize this, we need to practice self-observation. We need to relentlessly observe how we behave. We need to constantly assess the real drivers behind the decisions that we make. This has to be taken up without a break; there should be no time-off from observing the mind.

If we are not alert about our choices, then choices arise from our past programming, our pre-conditioning. The belief systems and behavioural patterns of people around us have had a deep impact on our subconscious mind since our formative years. If we are not alert, then our preconditioning shapes our future; we then lead a mechanical life like robots.

When a person fails in a job interview and gets disappointed, he does not realize that he is actually choosing to be unhappy. Even the choice of being unhappy ordains a future! Choosing to be unhappy is certainly not a higher choice. But, out of ignorance, most people unconsciously continue to make this choice day after day.

One who is vigilant about one's choices will decide to remain happy, despite such failure. In the frame of happiness, he treats his failure as a stepping stone to success. Such a higher choice will yield a bright future. What would your choice be in such a situation?

An alcoholic or drug addict may choose to linger in the abyss of unconsciousness. Another addict may decide to visit a rehabilitation centre to overcome his addiction. Each one of them is choosing their future based on their level of awareness in the given situation. We can clearly see that the one who decides to undergo rehabilitation is making the highest choice in the given situation. The other one who decides to remain steeped in intoxication is making a lower choice. He is choosing to create a hell for himself, while the other paves the way for a better future.

As with the minor, so it is with the major

If one chooses to watch a football match on TV when he is supposed to follow his daily exercise regimen, he ends up skipping his exercises. After the match, he may choose to have breakfast, after which it may not be possible to exercise the body. In this way, the mind unconsciously postpones the exercises for the next day. However, if he chooses to stick to his exercises despite all other distractions, then this is the highest choice.

You may wonder how daily consistent exercises can be the highest choice. It seems such a trivial thing. How can the highest choice apply in such minor matters? But the truth is that if we are able to make the right choices in minor or trivial matters, then our choices will naturally tend to be the highest in major or vital matters.

If we are unable to make appropriate choices in trivial matters, how then can our key choices be right? As with the minor, so it is with the major. We need to be alert and ensure that we make the right choices regardless of whether the context is trivial or vital.

Easy options can be deceptive

True progress in life occurs when man exerts himself against the forces of his tendencies and programmed behavioural patterns. However, given a chance, man tends to follow the path of least resistance and obeys the law of inertia. In order to avoid changing his predisposition, he flows with the tide of his tendencies by adopting shortcuts wherever possible.

Man falls prey to the temptations of sense gratification, of earning easy money; he rushes for quick fixes, and gives lame excuses without realizing it. To earn fast bucks, many people resort to illegal and immoral practices. One cannot avoid the consequences of such shortcuts for long. Such a life that is based on lower choices of a weak character inevitably leads to the doldrums.

Easy options may be enticing when viewed superficially. One may avoid exerting oneself when thrown into situations by choosing easier options, but there is a high likelihood of losing one's way by falling into the trap of such choices.

Whenever we are at a juncture where we need to take a major decision, we often find ourselves in a dilemma and feel tempted to choose easy options. We may likely choose not to make any decision as we fear the consequences. Even choosing not to decide brings its own future.

To avoid falling into the deception of easy options, we should be very clear about why we are choosing a given option. We need to ask ourselves the right questions.

1. Are our choices driven by the need to resist change and remain in our comfort-zone?
2. Are we choosing impulsively to escape situations or challenges?
3. Are our choices driven by the genuine will for inner growth and capability development?

Your choices – a reflection of who you are

If someone insults you, then how do you respond? The other person is expressing who he is by passing insulting remarks. Your response is a reflection of who you are.

The choices that we make in life serve as our reflection. It shows who we consider ourselves to be, whilst making the choice. The inability to make decisions indicates a weakness of character and a lack of conviction about one's real identity.

We need to ask ourselves, 'Who am I considering myself to be when I am making this choice?' This will help raise our awareness in the *interval of choice of response*. Let us understand the interval of choice of response. The moment you perceive any situation in your daily life, a thought occurs within you. If you impulsively react to this thought without a pause, your response is just a mechanical play of your past mind programming.

There is always a small time gap between the occurrence of the situation or event and the arising of the associated thought within you. This gap is the interval of freedom of choosing the right response. You can choose the right response by being consciously present in this gap.

If you are vigilant in this gap or you have practised enough to be conscious in this gap consistently, you will ask yourself, "Where is my response arising from? Is it from my past conditioning? Or is it a fresh response arising from pure awareness?" If you deviate even a little from that gap, then your response becomes a mechanical reaction and you end up losing your freedom.

Making the highest choice may initially require some effort to overcome inertia, to set oneself free from the shackles of prior conditioning. First, we need to at least try that 2 out of 10 choices that we make in the day are arising from higher awareness. The confidence that arises from being able to do this helps in increasing this to 4 of 10, then to 8 of 10. It will not be long before all our choices arise from the highest consciousness.

When you consistently make the highest choice, then life becomes a natural expression of gratitude and bliss. Soon, you will find that higher choices begin to naturally flow from within. You will naturally keep away from lower or mediocre choices. Dilemmas of the past will give way to a sense of gratitude and clarity of purpose.

When you have many options to choose from and you choose one option by weighing the pros and cons, before finalising that option, you need to consult your heart and request guidance from your innermost core, from your deepest being. Spend a few minutes in silence after making your choice. You will receive guidance intuitively through feelings, visuals, or words.

The next chapter outlines an effective meditation practice, which can help in identifying how we have made our choices in the past and help us in being more aware of our choices for for the future.

■

8

Decision Meditation

Since childhood, till the very end of life, each one of us keeps taking decisions. We are constantly making choices. Some decisions go well and some go wrong. The key question is: What does one assume oneself to be while making a choice? The underlying assumption about who-we-are, reflects in our decisions.

When we are not clear about who-we-truly-are, we allow our habits and beliefs to define ourselves. We hold onto the self-image that has been shaped through our habits and beliefs. We assume that we *are* this image. We then unknowingly find reasons to safeguard this self-image that we identify with. Changing our habits and beliefs seems to threaten this definition of who-we-are. Hence, it is important to look within and develop conviction about our true essence – who we are, and why we are.

People cite various reasons to justify the decisions they make. However, it is possible that the real reasons lie buried deep within us. Very often, our decisions arise from past conditioning. The real reasons why we make certain choices remain hidden in the dark, until they are brought to light.

The practice of meditation is an effective way of delving deeper into the inner working of our mind. We throw the light of awareness on the underlying impulses, tendencies and beliefs that make up this self-image. Through meditation, we can understand what are the real influencers for our choices.

We can introspect our past decisions to understand the building blocks of this self-image that we hold onto so dearly. By studying our past decisions, we can understand who we were assuming ourselves to be, when we made those choices. By witnessing from the standpoint of pure awareness, we can bring clarity into how our decisions could be, if we are not swayed by our conditioning.

Let us now consider the steps for such an introspective meditation, which can be called Decision meditation. You can first read through the steps and if required, record it, so as to play it back and actually practice it.

1. Set the timer for 15 to 20 minutes. Close your eyes and be seated in a relaxed posture. Let your spine be straight and upright, but not too stressed, so as to avoid fatigue.

2. Keep your body still and listen to the sounds around you. Identify at least five different sounds. Don't rush through this. With a quiet mind, focus your attention on each sound without paying special attention to any single one. Identify each sound and then move on to the next.

3. With each sound, there are other subtle sounds. Listen to them attentively: conversations of people, clattering dishes, children playing, the running engines of vehicles,

objects falling. Depending on where you are seated, you may also hear other sounds like footsteps, the TV, music, chirping of birds, dogs barking, water flowing, whistling, someone laughing, or a child crying. These are examples of ordinary sounds around us.

4. As you're listening to the various sounds, notice the presence of your own awareness in which these sounds arise. Ask yourself, "Who is listening to these sounds?" The answer will arise within you: "I am". Repeat the words 'I am' a few times and dwell in the feeling of 'I am'. This phrase anchors you in the space of presence of the one who is knowing these sounds.

5. Next, watch your breath. Feel the air passing through your nostrils as you inhale and exhale. If your attention strays, bring it back to your breath. See whether the breath is shallow, deep, or heavy. Howsoever your breath may be, know it without attaching any labels or trying to regulate it.

6. As you notice your breath, notice the presence of your own awareness in which the breath is arising. Ask yourself, "Who is noticing the breath?" Repeat the phrase a few times, 'I am' as an anchor to place you in the space of presence of the one who is knowing the breath.

7. Now turn your attention to your body. If there is stiffness or pain in any part of your body, notice the exact sensation. Be aware of the various sensations in your body. Which areas feel light or heavy? Which areas itch, are dry, or sweat?

8. While you are noticing your body sensations, also notice

the one who is knowing these sensations. Now shift your awareness to the one who is knowing by repeating the words 'I am' as an anchor. Abide in the presence in which these sensations are being felt.

9. Next, shift your attention to thoughts. After noticing a thought, let it go. There is no need to pursue it. Now watch the next thought.

10. After watching your thoughts for some time, ask yourself, "Who is knowing these thoughts?" The answer will arise, "I am." Know the knower of these thoughts. Repeat the words 'I am' as an anchor and continue being in this state. Rest in this feeling of the conscious presence that is knowing these thoughts.

11. Now, look at the various decisions that you have made from morning till now. Let every decision come to light.

12. With every decision that you've made, ask yourself, "Have I assumed myself to be the body, or the mind? Or have I made choices by knowing the 'I am' – the pure presence that I truly am?"

13. Take your attention to the events of your childhood. When you were a baby, you used to be in the cradle. After some days, you learned to walk and then you started going out of your house to play. Recall those situations. Try to see when you made some of your first decisions during childhood. It could be very trivial. A decision to play, to study, to compete with someone.

14. Move your attention further to your kindergarten days… then the initial years at school… the summer vacations…

in the house... in the market... with friends... with your siblings... on a picnic... Look at the decisions that you have made. Consider even the little trivial decisions. Keep recalling your decisions.

15. Did you make these decisions or did people decide for you? Sometimes you decided not to decide. What were the conclusions and beliefs that you had drawn from these incidents? Whatever they may be, just observe each decision and move onto the next.

16. Moving further from your childhood, now consider the decisions you made as a teenager. Repeat the introspection.

17. Recall the choices you made at home, in school or college, with friends, while shopping, with children, with elders, while you helped people, while doing household work. Look at those decisions and ask yourself, "What did I considered myself to be when I made those decisions? Did I assume this body to be me? Was I aware of the pure-witnessing presence that I truly am? What were my fears or needs that influenced those decisions?"

18. If you took the decisions considering yourself to be your body, what were the underlying tendencies that made these choices on your behalf? Was it fear, or guilt, or resentment, or greed? Whatever the tendency, know that it was with your body-mind, not you. Observe in a detached manner, without labelling them as good or bad.

19. Now, return to this moment. Ask yourself, "Who am I now?" Shift to the pure knower that is knowing everything

right now. Tell yourself: "I am not these thoughts. I am not this breath. I am not these body sensations. I am experiencing my conscious presence because of this body-mind."

20. Rest in this experience of 'I am' and decide how you will make decisions hereafter. Ask yourself, how you will make decisions in the future? Will you consider yourself as this body or the thoughts? Or you will make choices with the understanding of who-you-truly-are? How will you begin your day? How will you deal with people?

21. Slowly open your eyes. Reflect on the understanding that you've gained during this meditation session. Decide how you intend to make decisions hereafter.

During this meditation, you briefly come to experience your true nature, beyond the body-mind. You also get to know the basis for your past decisions. With this understanding, you can decide how you will make decisions in the future.

You would clearly recollect certain decisions, and you will need to spend more time to recollect some other decisions that you have made. Some deeper factors will become clear when you practice this meditation regularly. You will understand the tendencies that should not influence your decisions in the future. You will be alert about the precautions that you need to take? This will become clearer to you when you practice the meditation regularly.

While contemplating upon your past decisions, you will be able to identify the real drivers for certain past decisions that you were unaware of. You discover the ignorance of your true nature during the past decisions and can also identify the tendencies that influenced your choices. Bringing these to light will help in transforming your future decisions.

When you take decisions by being who you truly are, these new decisions will welcome a bright future, which will be free from the clutches of tendencies and ignorance.

∎∎∎

You can send your opinion or feedback on this book to :
Tejgyan Foundation, Pimpri Colony, P. O. Box 25,
Pimpri, Pune – 411017 (Maharashtra), INDIA
email : mail@tejgyan.com

APPENDIX

TEJ GYAN... THE ROAD AHEAD

What is Tejgyan?

Tejgyan is the existential wisdom of the ultimate truth, which is beyond duality. In today's world, there are a lot of people who feel disharmony and are desperately trying to achieve some balance in an unpredictable life. Tejgyan helps them in harmonizing with their true nature, the Self, thereby restoring balance in all aspects of their life.

And then there are those who are successful but feel a sense of emptiness or void within. Tejgyan provides them fulfillment and helps them to embark on a journey towards self-realization. There are others who feel lost and are seeking the meaning of life. Tejgyan helps them to realize the true purpose of human life.

All this is possible with Tejgyan due to a very simple reason. The experience of the ultimate truth is always available. The direct experience of this truth or self-realization is possible provided the right method is known. Tejgyan is that method, that understanding. At Tej Gyan Foundation, Sirshree imparts this understanding through a System for Wisdom – a series of retreats that guides participants step by step.

Magic of Awakening Retreat

Magic of Awakening is the flagship self-realization retreat offered by Tej Gyan Foundation where participants gain access to the experience of the Self and learn to live in the present every moment. The retreat is conducted in two languages – Hindi and English. The teachings of the retreat are non-denominational (secular).

Participate in the *Magic of Awakening* retreat to attain the ageless wisdom through a unique and simple 'System for Wisdom' so that you can:

1. Live from pure and still presence allowing the natural qualities of Consciousness, viz. peace, love, joy, compassion, abundance and creativity to manifest.
2. Acquire simple tools to use in everyday life which help quieten the chattering mind, revealing your true nature.

3. Get practical techniques to gain access to pure presence at will and connect to the source of all answers (the inner guru).
4. Discover the missing links in the practices of meditation *(dhyana)*, action *(karma)*, wisdom *(gyana)* and devotion *(bhakti)*.
5. Understand the nature of your body-mind mechanism to attain freedom from tendencies and patterns.
6. Learn practical methods to shift from mind-centred living to consciousness-centred living.

This residential retreat is held for 3-5 days at the foundation's MaNaN Ashram amidst the glory of mountains and the pristine beauty of nature. This ashram is located at the outskirts of the city of Pune in India, and is well connected by air, road and rail. The retreat is also held at other centres of Tej Gyan Foundation across the world.

For retreats in English email: ma@tejgyan.com

For retreats in Hindi, contact +91 9921008060 or email mail@tejgyan.com

A Mini retreat is also conducted, especially for teens (14-17 years) during summer and winter vacations.

Register online for all the above retreats at www.tejgyan.org

MaNaN Ashram :
Survey No. 43, Sanas Nagar, Nandoshi gaon, Kirkatwadi Phata, Sinhagad Road, Tal. Haveli, Dist. Pune 411024, Maharashtra, India.
Contact No.: 992100 8060.

About Tej Gyan Foundation

Tej Gyan Foundation (TGF) was established with the mission of creating a highly evolved society through all-round self development of every individual that transforms all the facets of his/her life. It is a non-profit organization founded on the teachings of Sirshree. The foundation has received the ISO Certification (ISO 9001:2008) for its system of imparting wisdom. It has centres all across India as well as in other countries. The motto of Tej Gyan Foundation is 'Happy Thoughts'.

TGF is creating a highly evolved society through:

- Tejgyan Programs (Retreats, Courses, Television and Radio Programs, Podcasts)
- Tejgyan Products (Books, Tapes, Audio/Video CDs)
- Tejgyan Projects (Value Education, Women Empowerment, Peace Initiatives)

The foundation undertakes various projects to elevate the level of consciousness among school students, youth, women, senior citizens, teachers, doctors, leaders, organizations, police force, prisoners, etc.

❖ ❖ ❖

Books can be delivered at your doorstep by registered post or courier. You can request for the same through postal money order or pay by VPP. Please send the money order to either of the following two addresses:

WOW Publishings Pvt. Ltd.

1. Registered Office: E-4, Vaibhav Nagar, Near Tapovan Mandir, Pimpri, Pune 411017.

2. Post Box No. 36, Pimpri Colony Post Office, Pimpri, Pune 411017.

Phone No. : 9011013210 / 9623457873

YOU CAN ALSO ORDER YOUR COPY AT THE ONLINE STORE:

Log in at: www.gethappythoughts.org

*Free Shipping plus 10% Discount on purchases above Rs. 300/-

The Source™ SERIES
For a Balanced Life

10 Million copies sold of The Source Series

Read the Source series to attain a balanced life, comprising 3 key facets: Mastery of Mind, Physical Vitality and Fulfilment at Work.

The Source
Access the Source of Love, Joy and Peace

Discover the Source of creation within you… Realize the 7 Powers of the Source in daily life… Leverage the 7 Laws of Thought to achieve mastery of the mind.

The Source of Health
The Key to Perfect Health Discovery

Discover the connection between your mind and body and how they relate to consciousness. Learn 7 principles and 7 tools to transform your physical health.

The Source @ Work
A Story of Inspiration from Jeeodee

Understand the principles of natural communication and effortless productivity through a story. Enjoy, energize and elevate your work with cues from this story.

Other Related Books

ISBN :
978-93-86618-27-6
Pages : 228
Published by :
Pentagon Press

The Secret of Awakening

This book is a compilation of profound answers that arise from the quintessence of wisdom.

What is the purpose of human life? What is wrong with desiring the fruit of our actions? What is the purpose of relationships? Is it spiritually wrong to pursue and acquire money? If God exists, why can't we see him? If God is perfect, what was the need to create an imperfect world? How can I free myself from the clutches of my past?

The answers to these questions and more, asked by seekers of truth and answered by Sirshree, unravel the deepest truths of life, dissolving our dilemmas and revealing the essence of spirituality.

ISBN :
9788-184-153-026
Pages : 208
Published by : WOW Publishings Pvt. Ltd.

Ultimate Purpose of Success

Success is your nature and you are programmed for success. From this premise, you can happily begin the journey of Complete Success. When you achieve material success, develop all your skills, and also achieve spiritual growth, that's when you attain Complete Success. And that's exactly what this book will help you to achieve. That's not all. When you spread your joy and inspire others to attain complete success, that's when you fulfil the Ultimate Purpose of Success. So, go ahead and fulfil it. The world is waiting for you.

For further details contact:

Tejgyan Global Foundation

Registered Office :

Happy Thoughts Building, Vikrant Complex, Near Tapovan Mandir, Pimpri, Pune 411017, Maharashtra, India.
Contact No.: 020-27411240, 27412576
Email: mail@tejgyan.com

MaNaN Ashram :

Survey No. 43, Sanas Nagar, Nandoshi gaon, Kirkatwadi Phata, Sinhagad Road, Tal. Haveli, Dist. Pune 411024, Maharashtra, India.
Contact No.: 992100 8060.

Hyderabad: 9885558100, **Bangalore:** 9880412588, **Delhi:** 9891059875, **Nashik:** 9326967980, **Mumbai:** 9373440985

For accessing our unique 'System for Wisdom' from Self-help to Self-realization, please follow us on:

	Website	www.tejgyan.org
	Video Channel	www.youtube.com/tejgyan
	Social networking	www.facebook.com/tejgyan
	Social networking	www.twitter.com/sirshree
	Internet Radio	http://www.tejgyan.org internetradio.aspx

Online shopping
www.gethappythoughts.org

Please pray for World Peace along with thousands of others at 09:09 a.m. and p.m. every day.

www.ingramcontent.com/pod-product-compliance
Lightning Source LLC
LaVergne TN
LVHW040157080526
838202LV00042B/3204